PRINCESS, UNICORN, FAIRY, AND MERMAID

CUTE COLORING BOOK
FOR KIDS AGES 4-8

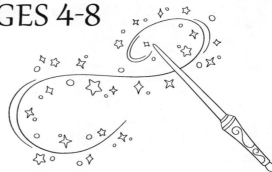

BEFORE YOU BEGIN...

If you use markers or highlighters, the ink may bleed through the paper and stain the next page.

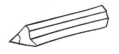

To prevent this, it is suggested to place a blank sheet of paper or two underneath the page you color.

Happy Coloring!

This Coloring Book Belongs to:

_____

_____

Made in the USA
Las Vegas, NV
03 November 2024

11093052R00052